BADGER THURSTON and the Cattle Drive

By
Gus Brackett

Illustrations by
Don Gill

Twelve Baskets Book Publishing
Three Creek, Idaho

Twelve Baskets Book Publishing, LLC
48600 Cherry Creek Rd.
Rogerson ID 83302
www.12bookbaskets.com
gus@12bookbaskets.com

ISBN-13 97809841876-0-7
ISBN-10 09841876-0-x

Author photo by Jill Davidson, Emotion Portrait Design
Edited by Dawn Geluso
Design by Chantel Miller

Other books in this series:
Badger Thurston and the Runaway Stagecoach
Badger Thurston and the Mud Pitts
Badger Thurston and the Trouble at the Rodeo

Table of Contents

Illustrations

Map

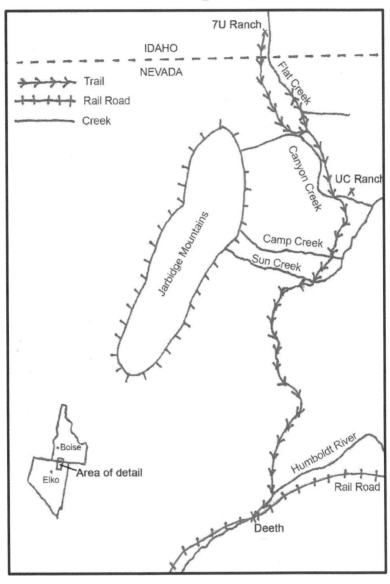

Chapter One

A THUNDEROUS BOOM BREAKS the dark silence. Badger Thurston scans the hillside and returns his focus to the four hundred steers he is guarding. A second BOOM shouts out, making the lazy steers nervous. Badger's big, brown horse dances and points his muley ears toward the noise. KB swishes his long, black tail as his black mane flaps in the breeze. KB paws the ground with his oversized hooves.

"Easy, KB," Badger says to calm his horse. "Easy. It's just thunder ... at least, I hope it's just thunder."

Lightning in the distance brightens the night sky. Fluffy rain clouds pass in front of the full moon. KB turns his nose, ears, and eyes toward the dark hillside. Lightning flashes again, and Badger sees where KB is looking. In the short brightness,

1

the young cowboy sees the dark outline of two riders on horses. As the darkness rushes back in, Badger squints his eyes to see them, but he can't see anything now. Lightning flashes again, but the two men are gone.

As Badger rides around the herd of steers, the wind blows. Badger sees the rough outline of his fellow cowboys asleep under a tarp back at the wagon. They sleep restlessly, awaiting their turns at night watch. The nervous steers all turn their heads into the wind. The moon and stars disappear completely behind the stampeding rain clouds.

The wind blows again, shrieking with fury. The willows bend and sway. The aspen trees' leaves rustle together, and their branches creak loudly. Badger pulls his coat around his neck to protect him from the cold air. The night sky flashes again, and thunder roars. Badger's eyes are wide open, and he breathes faster. Badger looks at the clouds and blinks as a big raindrop lands on the brim of his hat. Instantly, the night changes from calm to violent. Rain bombards Badger as lightning strikes the ground in the distance. Badger circles the herd, trying to calm the steers. A bolt of lightning strikes one hundred yards from the herd as a thunderclap rings through Badger's skull. A puff of smoke rises from the strike site, and the steers bolt like a runaway stagecoach, stumbling through the brush and charging toward the trees. As Badger presses his spurs to KB's flanks and gallops after the herd, he hears his name being shouted in the distance.

"Badger! Badger!" Gib cries as he chases

after the young cowboy.

Badger stops KB and waits for Gib. Gib still has sleepy eyes, and his round face stretches with a yawn as he approaches Badger. Gib pulls back on his braided reins and stretches his tall frame as his horse stops.

"Let 'em go," Gib says. "You can't stop a scared herd. We'll get 'em in the mornin'."

Together, the cowboys turn toward the buckaroo wagon, and Gib rubs his eyes.

"Get some shut eye," he tells Badger. "We're gonna have a long day tomorrow."

THE SUN PEEKS OVER the mountains on the eastern horizon. A Japanese man named Gordie cooks eggs, biscuits, and bacon. An apron covers his brown pants and brown vest. Gordie tugs on a silk scarf, which sports a tiger image that stretches from corner to corner. He adjusts a small, gray derby hat as he stirs their breakfast in his cast-iron pot.

As the coffee boils in another pot, an older man named Horace scowls at his aching joints. Horace combs his Santa Claus beard with his fingers and adjusts the straps on his overalls. He pulls his big, floppy hat up. It looks like he used the squashed hat for a pillow.

Badger opens his eyes as his friend Percy shakes him. Percy pulls his slightly used, gray hat down to his narrow eyes. His brown boots are as neat and new as his too-long chaps. He adjusts his loose-fitting blue shirt over his scrawny body as he eyes his friend to make sure he's really awake.

Badger blinks hard and rubs his tired eyes. His real name is Lawrence, but everyone calls him Badger because he looks a lot like a badger. He has a long nose, round cheeks, and big front teeth. His bit of pudge jiggles when he walks. Badger quickly rolls out of his bedding as he hears the cow boss talking about him.

"I don't think we should wake him up," Kenny gripes. "Every time we rely on Badger, somethin' goes wrong. I think we'd be better off without him."

"He tries hard," Gib says, defending Badger.

Gib buttons his brown vest and pulls on knee-high, leather boots as he talks. He takes great pride in wearing a cowboy costume. His big, brown hat is perfectly shaped. His shirt is bright red, and a yellow scarf is tied loosely around his neck. Gib is young, but he is still six years older than Badger.

"Losin' the herd wasn't my fault," Badger says, his voice tight from the cold night air. "It wasn't just the storm that spooked the steers. There were two guys scoutin' the herd. I think they're after the steers."

"Are you with 'em?" Kenny asks with a sneer.

Kenny looks mad, but he always looks mad. The cow boss is dressed in a black hat, black boots, and a black vest. Kenny reties his purple scarf and buttons the top button of his plaid shirt. A black handlebar mustache, piercing black eyes, and a natural scowl complement his meanness and anger.

"If I were with 'em, we'd be gone last

night," Badger says with his brow furrowed and hands on his hips. "I'm not the best cowboy, but I'm not a thief!"

"You're right about bein' a bad cowboy," Kenny says, "and that's enough to get this herd rustled."

"Well, I'm not a thief, and I'm not leavin'," Badger says as he crosses his arms and turns away from Kenny. Badger shivers as his anger and the cold morning's chill seize him.

"Eat in a hurry," Kenny tells the others. "We need to get movin'."

THE FIVE COWBOYS START the second day of this five-day cattle drive more sore and tired than normal because of the stormy night. They fan out around the scattered herd to gather the steers, which turn and march up the hill like tiny black and red ants up an anthill. They aren't as playful as they were the first morning. The burly beasts walk out of the small valley and follow a narrow trail near the top of a deep canyon. They trickle onto a rocky flat. The herd winds through rocks and short brush. Gib is in the lead, while Kenny and Horace push the sides, and Badger and Percy trail behind.

The cowboys yawn as the steers trudge beside Black Springs Canyon. The trail meanders between a sheer cliff to the north and a steep dirt cliff to the south. Kenny and Gib herd about forty steers along the path, and the rest of the herd dutifully follows the leaders. With a narrower trail, Horace joins Percy and Badger behind the drag.

The steers walk carefully over the rocks, around boulders, and through sagebrush.

"I'm warmin' up a bit," Badger says as he rubs his still-damp sleeve.

Horace chuckles and says, "If you get wet out here, you'll be cold for days. It seems like I'm only warm on a hot day. You know, I'm never just right. It's either too hot or too cold."

"I know what you're talkin' about," Badger says with a nod.

As the three stalk the herd, Percy eyes the older man.

"Why are you a cowboy, Horace?" Percy asks. "Most folk your age have long since settled down and started farmin'."

"I tried farmin'," Horace replies. "I had forty acres, a nice little home, and a pretty wife. But Wilda and the baby died in childbirth. It was lonely stayin' on the farm. So here I am, thirty years later, livin' like a wanderin' gypsy."

Horace sighs, rubs his eyes to stop any tears, and forces a grin. The cowboys return their focus to the steers with their thoughts churning in the silence.

"I thought bein' a cowboy would be fun," Badger says as he crosses his eyes. "Isn't bein' a cowboy fun, Horace?"

"I wouldn't say fun. It's a good life, though," the white-haired man replies. "I complain about the weather and about my aches and pains. We follow four hundred steers, and I'm still hungry most of the time. We're always eatin' sage chicken, rattlesnake, or jackrabbit—and it always tastes like sagebrush. A few years ago, I ate watermelon. I could eat that every day. It's really sweet ... better than the berries we have around here. But it's not all bad. The air up here in the mountains is as pure and clear as anywhere. I love the smell of wet sagebrush after a rain, and I love the smell of pine trees and wildflowers. When you sleep outside, you get to see that the stars are bright and twinkle like gold   dust. There are places up here in these mountains that a feller only sees when chasin' stray steers. And I get to work with people like you two, and Gib and Gordie. And even Kenny."

"This job would be better without Kenny," Badger says with a scowl.

"Kenny ain't so bad. He just has a big job to do, and he needs our help to get it done."

As one steer strays, Percy slides out of the conversation to herd it back to the group.

"I think Kenny's worried about a lot of things," Horace continues. "I think he's worried about how shorthanded we are. And he's worried about storms slowin' us down and about gettin' these steers on the train in Deeth. And he's worried about those fellers you saw yesterday. He's worried about a lot of things. You'd be grouchy, too, if you had that much to worry about."

As Horace's words about worries on the trail sink in, Badger and Percy pick up their pace, criss-crossing behind the herd more quickly. The herd crests a small hill as the trail opens onto a mountainous plain. Horace leaves the drag to push the sides. Badger and Percy move quickly, but the herd refuses to be rushed.

The caravan of cattle and cowboys follows the trail into a little, treeless valley. Short sagebrush flanks the bowl-like landscape. As a breeze blows, the taller grasses sway like rippling water. Kenny and Gib stop their horses to talk together. The herd slows and grazes. A few steers drink from a small spring seeping water across the green valley floor. Horace dismounts, so Percy and Badger follow his lead and slide to the ground.

"I didn't get enough sleep last night," Badger says.

"I'm tired, too," Percy replies as his face contorts with a yawn.

The two tie their horses to short sagebrush. Badger lies under a sagebrush tall enough to shade his face. Percy can't find a sagebrush big enough, so he digs down to damp dirt for a cool bed. The two close their eyes and fall asleep.

As Badger sleeps, the shade moves. The sun pounds down on him like a waterfall crashing on rocks. A fly wiggles into Badger's nose. He wakes up with a snort and brushes his face. Badger blows his nose, spits, and coughs twice. He scrunches his nose as Percy rolls over from his slumber.

"What are you doin', Badger? I'm tryin' to sleep over here."

"Sorry. A bug flew up my nose. It's hard to sleep. Is it always like this out here, or have we just not figured it out yet?" Badger asks as he blows his nose again. "What are we doin' goin' on a cattle drive like this?"

"You were the one who needed the money," Percy replies. "You said it would be an adventure. You said we'd have fun. You know, a better question is, what am *I* doin' on this cattle drive?'"

"You're watchin' out for your best friend," Badger says with a smile. "My adventures always turn out better when you come along."

Percy stretches his arms high in the air and opens his mouth to a loud yawn. The young cowboys yawn and shake, shake and yawn, shedding their bodies of sleep. A gentle breeze swirls through the calm air. It breaks an eerie silence—an uncommon silence—a no-steers-close-by silence. Badger and Percy jump to their feet and look for the noisy herd. They strain their necks looking down the trail, but the herd is gone. Their horses are missing, too. They can't see the older cowboys. Badger and Percy are stranded in the middle of a valley with no food and a two-day walk back to the ranch.

"Gordie has oats in his wagon. If I were KB, that's where I'd go," Badger says. "I bet both horses walked back to the wagon."

"But where's Gordie at? Sometimes he's followin' behind us, and sometimes he's in front of us," Percy replies.

"This early in the day, I bet he's still behind us," Badger says. "If we walk back the way we came, we should find 'em ... shouldn't we?"

"But where'd the herd go?" Percy asks. "Last time KB ran off, the herd hadn't moved anywhere. Kenny and the others wouldn't leave without us, would they?"

"I don't know, but we better get walkin' if we wanna catch up."

Badger and Percy walk back the way they came. They march quickly as they search for their horses, the herd, and the other cowboys. Where could they be? With a jolt, Badger wonders about the two riders he saw last night?

Badger and Percy rush up the hillside. As they reach its crest, they see KB and Snowball grazing.

"Why does he keep wanderin' off?" Badger asks as he lifts his hat and scratches his head. "I think he's doin' it just to make me look stupid."

"Well, we found the horses, but we still don't know which way the herd is headed," Percy says as he grabs his lazy horse's reins.

"It'll be easy to track 'em," Badger says. "A herd of four hundred steers leaves a pretty big trail, and it kicks up a lot of dust. We'll just follow the steers' trail till we see a cloud of dust."

Badger and Percy shake the pebbles out of their boots, mount their horses, and ride to where they last saw the herd. Then they walk their horses in large circles like a couple buzzards as they search for signs of where the herd went.

"I think I found the trail," Percy yells to Badger.

Badger hurries over and looks at the tracks. The trail leads north, almost in the same direction they came from that morning.

10

"Why are they turnin' back?" Percy asks.

"I don't know. It doesn't make sense. I have a bad feelin' about this," Badger says.

Badger lifts his hat and runs his fingers through his hair. He shakes his head to dislodge a thought.

"Well, there goes the herd. We better follow it and see what's goin' on."

11

AFTER FOLLOWING THE TRACKS for about two miles, Badger and Percy see a cloud of dust in the distance. It's rising from a trail that leads to Flat Creek Canyon. The path meanders like a rattlesnake through aspen and willow trees as it drops into the deep-sided canyon. No one rides with the lead steers, but the canyon walls prevent the beasts from straying. Meanwhile, two unknown men follow behind the herd. One rider is chubby and pushes the steers in the drag. He looks more like a farmer than a cowboy. He doesn't wear a vest or chaps over his tattered shirt and pants. His hat is small and has a dark sweat ring around the top. The other man is lanky and looks more like a gambler than a cowboy. His shirt and pants aren't new, but they don't show the wear a working man's clothing would. He sports an unbuttoned wool vest and a small, clean hat. His scraggly red beard is in need of a trim.

"This doesn't make any sense," Percy says as he wrinkles his nose and squints his eyes. "Those are our steers, but those men aren't Kenny, Gib, and Horace. And why are they headed down the mountain? We just came that way."

"Percy, I bet those are the two guys I saw last night. They probably stole the herd while we were sleepin'. I'd guess they're goin' into this canyon so they won't be seen."

"Let's go find Kenny," Percy says.

"If we leave the herd, we might not find 'em again."

"But how would we get the herd back?"

"I don't know, but I'm sure we can," Badger replies forcefully.

"Come on, Badger! Our job is to push the drag, not save the herd. Let's go find the other guys."

"But if we don't get the herd to Deeth, we don't get paid."

"It's only fourteen dollars. Let's go, Badger."

"Okay, okay."

The two cowboys retrace their trail. After a couple miles, they see Gordie and the buckaroo wagon. Gordie has camp set up and is cooking lunch. Kenny, Horace, and Gib sit around the campfire.

"Those dirty dogs stole my best horse!" Horace yells as Badger and Percy approach.

"They got the herd while you two were sleepin'," Kenny says as he stares at the horizon. "They came over the hill with their guns drawn. It's not worth dyin' over. They took our horses and headed down the canyon. It looks like the ride's over."

"You're just gonna let 'em get away?" Badger whines as he shakes his head.

"There's nothin' we can do," Kenny replies. "We don't have horses. The only gun we have is Gordie's varmint rifle. They have a head start. How would we get the herd back? We'll walk back to the ranch, notify the sheriff, and form a posse to get these guys and our money."

"Get our money!" Badger exclaims. "What

about the herd?"

"They'll have the herd sold before we even get back to the 7U. We'll try to get what we can."

Badger shakes his head in frustration.

"If me and Percy get the herd back, do we get a raise?" Badger asks.

Kenny laughs like a howling coyote. His mustache isn't used to a smile, so he uses his fingers to pull some stray hairs back into place. Kenny pushes his hat back off his forehead and unbuttons his top shirt button. "Are you jokin'? Those men are armed. They'd kill you without a second thought. It's not worth it, kid."

"If me and Percy get the herd back, will you pay us fifty dollars each?"

"No, I won't even consider it." "How about thirty dollars?"

Percy fidgets like a hungry chicken. He looks at Badger with his eyes crossed and nose wrinkled.

Percy whispers to Badger, "I'm not goin' with you, Badger."

"Yes, you are. We can get the herd back. I know we can."

"We could get shot!"

"Percy, just trust me. If you help me drive the herd back here, I'll do all the dangerous stuff."

"Do you even have a plan?"

"Absolutely," Badger says as he squares his shoulders.

"Okay, but I leave when the shootin' starts."

Kenny laughs again. "Okay, buckaroo, thirty

14

dollars for each of you if you get the herd back here. It'd be worth the money just to get rid of you for a while."

"We'll be back by nightfall," Badger says with an angry smile.

Badger spins his horse around and rides toward the stolen herd. Percy timidly follows behind his friend.

"I wanna hear your plan, Badger," Percy says as they move quickly down the trail.

"I'm still workin' out the details," Badger says without looking at Percy.

Chapter Two

BADGER AND PERCY RIDE alongside Black Springs Canyon. They wind down into the heart of Flat Creek Canyon and follow a trail that hugs the narrow creek. They move quickly past willows and thick stands of aspen trees. The steep canyon walls tower above the boys, and a carpet of greenish sagebrush links the narrow canyon floor to the rocky ledge near the canyon's top.

The herd is kicking up a cloud of dust nearly a mile farther down the trail. Snowball and KB trot quickly, dodging rocks like jackrabbits running from a dog and charging through horse-high sagebrush. After a long run, the boys stop to rest their horses at a bend in the canyon.

"So, Badger, what's your plan?" Percy asks.

Badger cringes, avoiding eye contact with Percy. He looks down at the pebbles. Then he looks at the clouds, searching for an answer to his friend's question.

"I haven't worked out the details yet," Badger says.

"You told me you had a plan," Percy whines.

"Okay, my plan is to get the herd, get back to Black Springs, take the herd to Deeth, and collect my money."

"So this is just about money," Percy says with an angry glare.

"No, Percy, this is about finally doin' somethin' right," Badger says as he leans toward Percy, his eyes begging his friend to believe in him. "I've managed to do everythin' wrong on this ride. I fell off my horse the first mornin'. I lost KB twice."

"Three times, if you count this mornin'," Percy interrupts.

Badger grimaces.

"I made a fool of myself ridin' KB like he was part of the rough string."

"That's an honest mistake, Badger, his real name is Killer Boy," Percy says with a chuckle. "It was pretty funny watchin' you ride scared for the first few hours."

Badger gives Percy a withering look before continuing.

"I burned my pant leg in the campfire. I spilled Gordie's sack of beans. I lost the herd in the thunderstorm."

"But, Badger, not all that stuff was your

fault," Percy says.

"Well, Kenny thinks so, and I wanna prove to him and everyone else, includin' myself, that I can do somethin' right," Badger replies fiercely. "With your help, Percy, I can do this!"

Silence stretches between them. Percy kicks a rock and glares at Badger. A circling crow squawks in the distance, and KB lifts his tail to pass gas.

"I've got an idea," Badger says, breaking the uncomfortable silence. "Listen to this!"

Percy leans in close as Badger tells him his plan. Percy's narrowed eyes begin to loosen as he nods and smiles his approval. As Badger continues, though, Percy's smile slides off his face.

"Slick plan, Badger," Percy says, "but I don't think it'll work."

"What do you mean?" Badger says as he throws his arms in the air. "You said it was a good plan!"

"It is a good plan, but there's just you and me. We can't do all that stuff. You think you're ridin' with Tap Duncan or Diamondfield Jack? It's just me, Percy Reed. I can't fire a warnin' shot. Heck, Badger, I don't even have a gun!"

"Well, let's try it—everythin' but the warnin' shot," Badger urges as he pulls close to Percy. "We have nothin' to lose."

"Nothin' to lose, Badger? What about our lives? When you begged me to come on this ride with you, I didn't think I'd get killed!"

Badger's shoulders slump, and his chin

19

drops toward his chest. "All right, Percy. You go on back. I'll get the herd by myself. But if somethin' happens to me, tell my mom I'll miss her, and sell my saddle to pay my debt at the store. And tell Nettie McCorkle that she'll always be the girl for me. Be sure to bury me near the quaky grove. And sing 'Old Rugged Cross' at my funeral..."

Percy heaves a sigh, rolls his eyes, and says, "Fine, Badger, fine! I'm comin'—but I'm gone when the shootin' starts."

Percy shakes his head and follows behind Badger.

"Nettie McCorkle doesn't even know your name," Percy grumbles. Under his breath he adds, "Sometimes, I wish I didn't know your name either."

AFTER RIDING FOR ANOTHER half hour, Badger and Percy creep on horseback to the herd like a couple of wolves stalking sheep. The canyon walls are deep and dark, and a steep draw ascends up the western wall like a well-placed stairway. The rocky cliffs part near the top, and a small deer trail connects the chasm's bottom with its top. Badger pulls KB to a stop and turns to Percy.

"Here's the best place to get on top. You go on around to the front of the herd. I'll catch up to the drag," Badger says as his voice cracks.

Percy turns his horse up the trail and then hesitates.

"Ar-ar-are you sure you w-wa-wanna do this, Badger?" Percy asks.

20

"I'm sure I do, Percy. We're smarter than these guys. Our plan'll work. You just do as we agreed and be careful. Everythin' will work out," Badger says with a reassuring smile.

Percy and Snowball set out on the narrow deer trail, heading out of the canyon.

"How can this possibly work?" Percy mumbles to himself.

The things I do for Badger. Sometimes, I wonder why I call him a friend. Percy shakes his head and smiles. *Probably because he calls me his friend.*

As Percy moves away, Badger dismounts and ties his horse to a willow near the trailhead.

"You stay here," Badger says as he waggles his finger at his horse. "I need you to stay this time."

KB paws the ground and shakes his head. Badger inhales deeply and then begins hiking along the chasm's floor. As Badger approaches the back of the herd, he angles over to the western wall. The canyon is steep and rugged with twenty feet of vertical rock at its top. Badger groans. *Climbin' the dirt portion is gonna be tough*, he tells himself, *but you can do this.*

The young cowboy grabs fistfuls of sagebrush and begins hoisting himself up the canyon wall. He breathes heavily as the dust in the air cakes his sweaty face. Badger stops behind a bushy sagebrush about fifty yards from the drag. He can see the thieves clearly, but they can't see him. Badger gulps in air. His heart is pounding like a bass drum in a marching band. His hands shake, and his legs ache from the climb. He closes his eyes, not to sleep, but to think. He takes deep breaths to stop the burning in his lungs and legs.

Finally, Badger stands and squawks, "Hey, fools! I see where you are."

He gulps the squeak out of his voice and yells again. "I'm gonna tell the sheriff and collect your bounty. You clowns are as good as caught!"

Badger spits raspberries like an angry camel and waves his hands next to his ears. One of the cattle rustlers pulls out a pistol, aims hastily at Badger, and fires a quick shot. Badger hears a whizzing sound, sees a puff of dirt fly up about ten feet to his left, and hears the loud bang of the pistol firing.

Badger freezes. A part of his brain notes how strange it is that the bullet travels faster than the sound of the pistol firing, while a louder, more panicked part of his brain shrieks, *Run, you idiot, run!* Coming to his senses, Badger sets off up the hill like a blue-tailed lizard.

"Ike, he's just a kid. Don't kill him, catch him," the portly rustler tells his partner.

The rustlers chase Badger up the hillside. Badger's legs churn furiously, and sweat pours down his face. His lungs heave as he grabs onto sagebrush for balance. Badger reaches the canyon's sheer rock face. His fingers find handholds, and his toes wedge his boots into crevices. Then the young cowboy begins to climb.

The two thieves gain ground as they ride

their horses past the spot where Badger shouted. Their mounts dodge sagebrush as they jump and climb. About twenty yards from the rock face, their horses halt abruptly, winded from the steep climb. The rustlers dismount and chase Badger on foot.

Meanwhile, Badger shimmies along a narrow ledge like a circus tightrope walker. He presses his belly against the canyon wall to keep from falling. His hands shake as they search out new handholds. Finally, the ledge opens onto a thin trail, and Badger sprints twenty steps along flat ground. He suddenly stops midstride—arms windmilling— two feet from a narrow ravine. The chasm is about six feet wide and sixty feet deep. Badger quickly surveys his options. He scopes out the remaining vertical portion of the rock face; it offers no place to climb. He looks back and sees the two rustlers shimmying toward him. Badger's only chance of escape is to jump the ravine.

Badger takes several steps back and then runs at the abyss, jumping with all his strength. Badger's boot tip grabs the other side—and then slips. The young cowboy falls to his belly with his legs dangling into the gorge. The rocks give way, and Badger slides to his elbows. With the thieves climbing closer to the ravine, Badger wriggles his body back up the rocky edge. When his belly crests the ledge, Badger swings his legs to the right, finds a firm spot for his foot, and pulls himself to the top of the cliff. Just as the thieves reach the ravine, Badger gets to his feet and runs up a chute between two rocks, disappearing over the top of the canyon.

"That crazy kid," the pudgy thief wheezes. "He's gonna get us killed if we try to follow him."

The climb has Ike gasping and shaking. He stops at the edge of the ravine and pulls out his pistol, firing five wild shots in Badger's direction, but the teenage cowboy is long gone.

"Ike, you can't shoot a kid! You just can't," the hefty rustler yells.

"Joe, you dimwit," Ike retorts. "I swear you're as dumb as a fence post! If that kid reaches the sheriff, we're headin' back to prison. I can't live off prison slop; I've got no meat left to lose!"

Joe gulps. "You've gotta point there, Ike. I lost thirty pounds last time. Let's go around. We can still catch him."

Badger sees the two robbers turn around, but he doesn't slow down. He runs another hundred yards across the top of the canyon. He finally stops, rests his palms on his knees, and takes three big gulps of air.

He straightens up and yells, "Do it now, Percy!"

From a willow patch on the canyon floor, Percy and his horse dash out of hiding. Percy wildly waves a willow branch and yells, "BOO HAW!" like a scared rabbit as he gallops Snowball the short distance to the front of the herd. Already scared from the shooting, Percy's ruckus causes the lead steers to bolt, setting off a chain reaction through all four hundred beasts. A broad smile stretches across Badger's face. The herd is stampeding, just as planned.

Badger spots KB about halfway up the canyon—nowhere near where he left him. The proud teen finds a gentle slope and runs to KB, who is standing with five other horses. Badger recognizes Kenny's, Gib's, and Horace's mounts. Joe's and

Ike's horses are nearby, too. The young cowboy jumps into his saddle and herds all the horses, including the rustlers', to Percy. The frightened herd has knocked down many willows and sagebrush, sending up a massive cloud of dust.

"Okay, let's get goin'. We gotta get back to Black Springs before dark," Badger says as he nervously eyes their surroundings. "The others aren't gonna be there in the mornin'. And the two rustlers are on foot up on that ledge, but they'll eventually get down and be followin' us. We better hurry."

The frightened boys reach the startled herd about a mile up the canyon. The sun is just starting to head down, so Badger figures it must be about four o'clock. That means they have four hours or so of daylight to get the herd back to Black Springs. Most of the steers breathe like fat men climbing stairs. Their heads hang low, and their sides heave in and out. Their tongues dangle from their mouths as drool leaks out.

"Badger, the steers look pretty tired. We can't get 'em goin' when they're fresh in the mornin'; how are we gonna get 'em to Black Springs by nightfall?" Percy asks with eyes like a spooked antelope.

"I don't know," Badger says, "but we gotta."

THE HERD STROLLS ALONG the banks of Flat Creek. The lumbering animals measure their steps more carefully when tired, so the herd is almost at a standstill. Badger and Percy are worn out, too, but they encourage the herd to keep moving. They ride back and forth behind the herd. They wave their arms. They yell, they scream, and they whistle, but nothing compels the steers to get walking. The boys are about a mile and a half from where they left Kenny, Gib, and Horace.

"Maybe if we hide for a few minutes and then sneak up on the steers, they'll stampede again," Percy suggests.

"It's worth a try. If we can't get 'em movin', the thieves are gonna catch up to us—if they haven't already," Badger says with a gulp. "What if they're watchin' us now, Percy?"

The two cowboys hide KB and Snowball in a thicket of willows. They slowly stalk the herd like boys trying to scare their sister. They tiptoe from sagebrush to sagebrush, crouched where the steers can't see them. With Badger on the left side and Percy on the right, they slink within a few feet of the steers. Suddenly, the friends run at the steers, and Badger shrieks "YAWGEDY BOOGEDY!" while Percy slaps one steer on the rump. All the steers lift their tails in the air and stampede—for about fifty yards. Then almost as quickly as they stampeded, they stop and eyeball Badger and Percy. The steers have their ears pricked forward, and the meaner ones blow snot from their noses and paw the ground.

"I think we made 'em mad," Percy says.

Unconvinced, Badger waves his arms and jumps in the air to startle the herd again. One angry steer lowers his head and charges halfway to

Badger. The steer takes aim at Badger like a bull sizing up a matador at a bullfight. Badger stands his ground but prepares to run.

"Um, yeah...You're right, Percy. The stampede was a bad idea. I think we better get our horses," Badger says.

The two young cowboys walk quickly to their horses while watching the angry herd. Badger and Percy mount up, and the steers saunter up the canyon—one achingly slow step at a time.

"Maybe we should stop and rest for a little while," Percy says. He looks as frustrated as a fast mule hitched to a slow one.

The two dismount and settle like sage chickens under a sagebrush. They close their weary eyes, but find no sleep in the excitement. After about a half hour without sleeping, Badger jumps up and surveys the herd. The steers have grazed about a quarter mile up the canyon.

"They're startin' to move, Percy. Let's get 'em goin' again. Those rustlers are probably madder than wet hens by now, and they could be anywhere out there," Badger says as he peers over his shoulder. "What if they're just waitin' for dark to attack?"

The boys mount their horses and return to the herd. The steers gently graze as Badger and Percy make noise and move back and forth behind the drag. The steers ignore them, walking up the canyon only fast enough to eat.

After struggling with the beasts for three hours, Badger and Percy finally climb out of the

28

canyon. They have one last horizon to crest to reach the other cowboys, and there's less than an hour of daylight left. The trail opens to a dry meadow, and the herd fans out to eat some more. Badger and Percy try to keep the sides pushed in, but the edges expand around them. The hungry steers haven't spread out to graze all day, and now they're making up for it. The harder Badger and Percy try to keep them moving, the more the stubborn steers resist.

"Move, you stupid beasts!" Badger yells. "I think the steers are tryin' to get rustled again. If only there was a way to tell 'em we're bein' followed."

"We're so close. Why don't they wait till we top the next hill? The grass is greener and they'd be safer," Percy whines as a small tear escapes from the corner of his eye. "Why don't they just move?"

"All they know is they're hungry. Hunger's more powerful than fear, I guess," Badger replies. He peeks at Percy from under his lashes and says innocently, "Maybe you should stay with the herd while I go get the others. It's not far. It'll only take a half hour if I hurry."

"I don't think so, Badger," Percy growls. "Those two thieves are still behind us, and they still have guns. I'm not gonna wait here and be the target! This was your idea. I'll go. You stay here and watch the herd."

Badger opens his mouth to respond, but he is as silent as a statue. He's been jumpy and nervous for the past three hours, but now he is still. Percy's right, but Badger's scared.

"I was the one who provoked the rustlers.

They'd shoot me for sure," Badger says.

Percy responds forcefully, "I'm goin'! I'll take the horses back to camp. You can come, too, and hope the herd stays ... or you can stay and watch 'em."

Badger growls at Percy. Then he shakes his head and sighs.

"Okay, Okay. I'll stay. But you better hurry!"

Percy pulls out his rope to use as a lead line and ties the trailing horses' reins to it. Badger watches Percy's long shadow crest the horizon as the last sliver of sun drops in the west. Chills dance down his spine, and Badger feels as lonely as a skunk at a dance hall. Fear seems to be his only riding partner now.

Chapter Three

BADGER PULLS THE SADDLE off KB to air the horse's back. The brown horse is caked with sweat. As KB grazes, Badger crawls under a thick sagebrush. He tells himself it's because he needs to rest, but really he just wants the heart-pounding fear to go away. The young cowboy's body trembles, and the sound of the sagebrush rustling makes him as jumpy as a scaredy-cat. He shifts to his left and turns to his right. He tosses a rock away and brushes back some stickers.

I've gotta get control of myself, Badger thinks.

He tries to sing, but his thirsty voice cracks and skips like a scratched record on an old-time record player. He tries to whistle, but his parched lips release no sound. Now he understands why Gib carries a harmonica. Badger crawls from the sagebrush and grabs his saddle.

"If I can't sleep, I'll just keep the herd movin'," he says to no one in particular.

The gray dusk swallows the long shadows sunset casts. The anxious teen resaddles KB and presses the drag. The steers move forward, but only to eat fresh bunches of grass. As the sky darkens, Badger squints at his surroundings more than he watches the herd. Shadows and darkness trick Badger's eyes. Every sagebrush looks like a cattle rustler, and every rock seems to be a coiled snake ready to strike. KB pays no attention to the potential threats, but Badger's imagination makes these fears seem very real.

Badger jumps at every shadow like a scared kid on Halloween. Clouds roll in, partially blocking the moon and stars. Badger finds himself in total darkness, and fear throbs through his body. He stalks the steers to herd them forward. The steers refuse to budge, but the motion soothes Badger's nerves.

Another five minutes of darkness pass. The brown-haired teen sits in stillness atop his horse. Suddenly, the hairs on the back of Badger's neck stand up. KB snorts and turns to look behind his rump. The steers look in the same direction as KB. Their ears perk forward, investigating the sound of a potential predator.

"I don't like this, KB. I wish Percy and the others would get here," Badger whispers hoarsely.

KB nods his head and paws the ground. Badger looks in the same direction as the animals.

He sees a flash about forty yards away and hears a bullet whiz near his head, followed by the loud crack of a gun. The noise startles KB, who jumps like a leaping lizard, flinging Badger off his back. Badger's voice catches in his throat, too frightened to scream. He thumps face-first into a patch of sagebrush, which breaks his fall. KB bucks twice more and then settles.

"I shot him, Ike," Joe says smugly. "Let's go get his horse and get outta here."

"Are you sure you shot him, Joe? I can't see a thing in this dark."

"I don't care. Even if he's armed, he probably can't shoot, and I'm not movin' another step without a horse."

Badger tries to suck in air as he lies on his back amid three sagebrush that shelter him from sight. He feels his head, arms, and torso to make sure the rustlers are wrong about the shooting. Besides some soreness in his back and rump, Badger feels fine, and none of his body is sticky with blood. Badger waits silently.

The two thieves walk quickly over to KB, who has lowered his head and is grazing.

"I'll ride in front; you ride in back," Ike tells Joe.

"Wait a minute. I shot the kid. I should get the reins."

"Okay, okay," Ike says.

Joe, a short man shaped like a pear, bounces to get his foot into the stirrup. He strains and grunts as he pulls himself into the saddle. Ike saunters to

33

KB and reaches for the left stirrup. Tall and thin, he swings easily onto KB's rump, landing a bit awkwardly behind the saddle.

"Are you settled?" Joe asks.

Ike mumbles yes, and Joe kicks KB in the belly. KB casually lifts his tail and passes gas. Joe kicks the horse again—this time harder. KB yawns a horse yawn. Joe mutters under his breath, swings the ends of the reins, and whips the horse's flank.

KB lifts his head, snorts, and jumps high in the air. As the large beast drops to the earth, he kicks both hind hooves. A cloud of dust rises where KB once was. After another small jump, KB gathers his hooves under him and leaps again. As the crafty horse thumps back to the ground, the impact catapults Ike from KB's rump. With arms flailing, Ike somersaults and dives head-first into a pile of rocks. Still atop KB, Joe's knuckles are white as he clutches the saddle horn.

KB hops around like a toady frog. He throws his front legs to the left and kicks his back legs to the right. KB and Joe both grunt, snort, and oink through the entire affair. Following KB's impressive theatrics, the plump cowboy slides out of the saddle and plops to the ground. KB then walks casually away from the offending lump, takes two deep breaths, and begins grazing again.

Except for some short, easy breaths, Ike lies motionless amid the rocks. A few feet away, Joe groans, his body twisted on the ground. Badger jumps from his hiding spot and jogs to KB. He retrieves his rope from the saddle and unwinds

one end. He walks to Joe, who is writhing in pain, and throws the rope over his upper body. Joe looks stunned as Badger pulls the rope tight. Badger loops the rope around the rustler again and ties it off.

"You're supposed to be dead! I shot you," the pudgy thief says in disbelief.

With Joe's arms tied, Badger walks to the bandit's side and pulls his pistol out of its holster. "So this is the gun that almost shot me ...twice," Badger says angrily as he aims the gun at Joe.

"No, no, no!" Joe squeals as his face turns white. "Ike shot at you the first time."

Badger cocks the gun, which is still aimed at the thief.

"W-w-we weren't tryin' to kill you. That's why we m-m-m-missed," Joe stammers with his lips quivering like a bawling baby. "We just w-w-wanted to scare you. Don't shoot me, kid. I'm not worth it."

Badger moves the gun slightly to the left and squeezes the trigger. The barrel flashes and the gun thunders. A small cloud of dust rises next to the thief.

Badger shakes his head.

"I'm not tryin' to kill you. That's why I missed," Badger says, measuring his words carefully. "I just wanna scare you."

Joe sobs loudly. Tears stream down his dirty cheeks, and his head hangs in shame. His whole body shakes with fear. Badger keeps his eyes on the thief.

"You better keep your mouth shut, stranger. My aim might be better next time," Badger says with his teeth clenched.

Badger quickly binds Joe's feet; then he ties the tail of the rope around the unconscious Ike. Badger pulls Ike's gun out of its holster, too. With the two thieves secure, Badger sits down near KB. He closes his eyes, not to sleep, but to calm his frayed nerves. He breathes deeply and silently begs Percy to bring help soon.

AS PERCY TOPS THE hill and runs into Black Springs, he hears a gunshot in the distance. He kicks Snowball to move faster, but the five horses he leads hamper him like an anchor slows a boat.

"We got the horses. We got the herd," Percy yells.

The three cowboys and Gordie are resting under the tarp.

"We got the horses," Percy yells again. "We got the herd back."

Still, no one moves. When Percy gets within fifty yards of the camp, he tries again, "KEEEEENNNNNYY! We got 'em. We got the horses and the herd!"

Kenny is the first to hear. He sees Percy, jumps to his feet, and runs to the skinny cowboy with Gib hot on his heels.

Percy talks quickly.

"We got the horses and herd. Badger's back with the steers, and the rustlers are armed and followin' him. They're on foot, but we've been movin' pretty slow."

Another gunshot rings out in the distance.

"We better help the kid out," Gib says as he swings up onto his horse.

"But we don't have guns," Kenny protests with his mouth wide open.

"Well, Badger was able to get the herd back this far without any gun, so the least we can do is help him," Gib says as he turns his horse and gallops away.

Kenny shakes his head as he mounts his horse.

"Crazy kids," he mutters. He turns to Percy.

"Tell Horace and Gordie what's goin' on," Kenny says, "and go get somethin' to eat."

GIB TOPS THE HILL and sees the herd in the darkness. He inhales to yell for Badger, but stops, remembering that the sudden noise would scare the steers. Gib rides around the herd. He sees Kenny topping the hill behind him. Near the back of the herd, Gib's horse stops like he hit a fence and jumps hard to the right. Gib, an experienced rider, stays planted in the saddle. He quickly dismounts to look for whatever spooked his horse.

"Badger, are you here?" Gib whispers. "Badger, is that you?"

"What? Who's there?" Badger asks as he raises one of the rustlers' guns.

"Don't shoot! Don't shoot! It's me, Gib," he says as he throws his hands in the air. "Wait a minute; where'd you get that gun, Badger? And stay down. Percy says those cattle rustlers are still around."

"Those cattle rustlers are tied up over there. And I got their guns after I tied 'em up," Badger replies as Kenny approaches.

"What's goin' on here?" Kenny asks. "Badger got the herd back. And he caught the thieves. They're tied up over yonder," Gib says as he points into the darkness.

"I'll be jiggered. Badger did all that? I'll be … but how'd you do it, kid?"

"I got 'em on foot with a chase, and they lost their horses in the stampede that Percy set up. After that, KB and Snowball did most of the work," Badger says as he kicks the dirt.

"I wouldn't believe it if I wasn't seein' it with my own two eyes," Kenny says, still shaking his head. "Badger, you head on back to camp and get some food and rest. Send Horace here with a couple horses. These two fellas need somethin' to ride to the sheriff's office in Deeth. Gib and I'll stay here and settle the herd before we come back. Good work, Badger. I completely doubted you, and you proved all of us wrong. You earned your money. And you earned my respect."

"Aw … it was nothin'," Badger says with a half smile.

As Badger and KB head back to camp, relief washes over him. A weary grin stretches across his face, and for the first time on his first cattle drive, Badger feels like a real cowboy.

Chapter Four

BADGER OPENS ONE EYE. Then he opens the other. He heaves himself up to lean on his elbow and looks around. Kenny is awake and collecting wood to fuel a breakfast fire. Everyone else, including the two tied-up thieves, is still asleep.

"You finally have your mind's clock set to cowboy time, Badger," Kenny says with a smile. "I didn't have to wake you up. I bet it won't take as long to work the stiffness outta your body this mornin'. It usually takes a couple days, but the body always adjusts."

Badger squints his eyes and tilts his head as Kenny speaks.

"Badger, Gib's still sleeping. He had a pretty long night last night. Why don't you wrangle the horses?" Kenny asks.

"Okay … but how? I've never wrangled

before."

"There's a bucket of oats in the back of the wagon. The horses usually come runnin' to the oats. Catch your horse, or one of 'em, and saddle him. Then herd the rest of 'em close by. Breakfast should be ready when you get back."

Bucket in hand, the blue-eyed youngster walks nearly a quarter mile to the horses. He shakes the oats, and the horses run to him like schoolkids to an ice-cream parlor. Badger saddles KB and climbs into his seat. Then he herds the remaining horses to the buckaroo wagon and the waiting cowboys.

Badger plops down next to the campfire as the others saddle their horses. He warms his cold hands near the flames. Gordie cooks their breakfast in a cast-iron pot next to the fire while the coffeepot bubbles and boils.

"I found some sage-chicken eggs yesterday, so we get eggs for breakfast," Gordie says proudly. "And I shot three jackrabbits. These rabbit steaks are tasty. Oh ... and the biscuits."

"Of course," Badger replies. "We always get biscuits. Gordie, why's it we're followin' four hundred fat steers and we're eatin' varmints for breakfast like a pack of coyotes?"

"Because steers are worth seven dollars, and rabbits are free. Beef steaks would be a very expensive breakfast."

"Where did you learn to cook rattlesnakes and rabbits and all the stuff we've been eatin'?" Badger asks Gordie between bites.

"When I first came to America, I worked

on a sugar-beet farm in Colorado. I didn't have anything or any money; so I either ate jackrabbit, or I starved," Gordie replies without looking up from his work.

"What about your name?" Badger asks. "I don't know any Japanese, but 'Gordie' doesn't sound at all Japanese."

"My real name is Kazu. At the farm where I worked, there were already two other guys named Kazu, so I needed a new name," Gordie says with a smile. "One of the first English words I tried to say was 'golly.' My English wasn't as good as it is today, though, and it came out 'gorry.' My boss added a 'd,' and I have been called Gordie ever since."

Badger eats with a smile as he thinks again about cowboys eating rabbit for breakfast. He wipes his face with his scarf and washes his plate in a nearby spring. Badger takes a pull on a second cup of coffee and gasps as the hot liquid burns his tongue. The thick, black coffee tastes disgusting, but it warms his belly.

Gordie wraps a biscuit and some jerky in a cloth and hands it to Badger.

"Take a little extra food with you," Gordie says. "The trail is too steep for a wagon, so I have to go around on the mining road. I won't see you again until after lunchtime."

"Are you takin' the rustlers with you?" Badger asks.

"They will be tied up in the wagon. They aren't very tough without their guns."

"Well, be careful with 'em," Badger says.
"Kenny thinks there's probably a reward if I get 'em to the sheriff."

"I'll do my best, but I am just a cook on a buckaroo wagon."

Badger climbs onto KB and rides to the bunching herd. He takes his place near the back next to Percy. The two young cowboys are tired, but their bodies are adjusting. As the herd moves down the trail, Kenny drops from his position to the drag.

"Badger, why don't you take my spot for a little while? I'd like to see how the drag is travelin' today," Kenny says.

"W-w-what? You want me—" Badger gulps. "I don't know what to do up there!"

Kenny stifles a smile.

"It's really pretty simple," he replies. "Just make sure the steers between Gib and Horace don't fan out and start grazin'. It only takes one to start grazin' before the whole herd gets the idea, so be vigilant."

"O-o-o-okay. I'll do my best," Badger says.

Badger chews on his lower lip nervously as he takes his new position. He is about halfway between Gib and Horace. Within moments, one steer stops to graze. It slows the herd behind it like a busted wagon on Main Street. The steer wanders off the trail. Badger moves close to intimidate it back into the herd. Just then another steer stops to eat. Badger pushes it back into the herd, too. Steers keep stopping to eat, and Badger works to keep them moving. *Am I doin' this wrong?* The teen wonders.

He looks over at Gib and Horace. The experienced cowboys are just as busy as he is. Badger had assumed riding the drag was the hardest job, but riding point seems just as difficult. *Not only is it tough, it's just as borin'*, Badger thinks sullenly. *The dust isn't as bad, though.* He can breathe more easily, and no dust lands on his hat, face, and shoulders. After about an hour, Percy rides to Badger at the middle of the herd.

"Hey, Badger. How's it goin'?" Percy asks as he approaches.

"Pretty good, but this is harder than it looks."

"Well, Kenny wants me to switch places with you. Kenny's in a good mood. He's as chatty as my Aunt Maude."

Badger smiles. "No one's as chatty as your Aunt Maude. She'd even talk to fence posts ... and go on and on about her bunions and her squash and that three-legged cat of hers and—"

"You're right, Badger," Percy interrupts with a chuckle. "Kenny's not that chatty."

Badger drops back to the drag. He moves back and forth, herding the steers. Badger keeps moving to avoid conversation.

"Hey, Badger," Kenny says as they zig together before zagging back apart.

"Hey, Kenny. How's it goin'?" Badger replies when they near each other again.

The conversation continues like this for some time. They speak for the thirty seconds they are close and are silent for the thirty seconds they

are apart. Badger is surprised by the length and
depth of their exchange. Kenny is friendly and

talkative. For the three days Badger has known him, Kenny has spoken to Badger only to scold him—until now. *Have I finally been accepted as a cowboy?* Badger wonders. *Probably not, but maybe this is a first step.*

"I remember my first cattle drive," Kenny says as his horse moves easily. "I was fourteen ... so about your age I guess. I remember bein' sore for a week. I wasn't used to long hours, so I was tired the whole time. But when the steers filed into the rail yard and the gates closed behind 'em, I've never been prouder of anythin' in my whole life. In the twenty-five years since then, closin' the gates on a cattle drive is the only time I get that old feelin'."

"Why'd you get started cowboyin'?" Badger asks.

"Same reason you did. The family farm didn't make enough to keep us goin'. I could either stay and everyone would be hungry, or I could get a job punchin' cows and all of us could survive."

The conversation pauses as they move apart. Badger hollers "HUP, HUP" and "WHOOP STEERS" and "GET 'EM UP" as he pushes the edges, encouraging the steers to continue up the trail.

"Badger, I really appreciate what you did yesterday," Kenny says as the two cowboys draw together and stop their horses. "You probably saved my job. Those steers may've been recovered, but they wouldn't be as fat and wouldn't be worth much. I owe you one."

Badger looks at the dirt as he searches for a response.

47

"Kenny, I'm sorry about all my mistakes. And I'm sorry for all the mistakes I'm gonna make between here and Deeth. But I want you to know that I'll try my best. No more naps," Badger says with a chuckle. "Just so you know, I didn't get the herd back for the money. What I did yesterday was to prove to everyone I could do somethin' right."

"I'll still pay what I promised," Kenny said, "and I bet there's a reward for the two robbers. This probably wasn't their first robbery."

Badger smiles like a gambler with four aces. The two sit briefly in silence, absorbing the meaning of their conversation.

"Kenny, I just got one more question." "Yeah, Badger?"

"Who named my horse Killer Boy? He's nothin' of the sort."

"I named him Killer Boy," Kenny says, guffawing loudly. "It's a little trick we play on rookies. You were scared of KB that whole first day."

Kenny's chest bounces as continues laughing.

"I see, I see," Badger says with a smile. "You got me on that one."

"Well, we better keep movin'," Kenny says as his serious demeanor quickly returns. "It looks like clouds are movin' in. We need to get over the ridge's top before it snows."

"Before it snows?" Badger asks. "It's August. It doesn't snow in August."

"It can snow up in the mountains in August.

48

I've seen it before, and I don't wanna see it again.
Let's get goin'."

Chapter Five

FROM BLACK SPRINGS, THE herd files into a narrow draw in the canyon. About two miles down the canyon, Gib turns the herd, and the steers head up a steep trail. After a short climb, the beasts walk to Buckhorn Ridge, which is flat and rocky. Short grasses grow in the gravelly soil, but no trees or brush break up the scenery. The ridge is framed between a deep canyon to the west and a steep cliff to the east. The steers pant heavily as they climb to the ridge's highest point. They trudge by twos in front and five across in back. Only the towering Jarbidge Mountains stands higher in the distance. As Badger tops the ridge, dizziness washes over him. He sways in his saddle, and the canyon swims before his eyes.

Soon, Gib dismounts and unsaddles his horse. He sits on the ground using his saddle as a backrest and loses himself in the sounds of his harmonica. Percy and Horace look for a comfortable spot and bed down next to each other. The late-morning sun is finally sharing some of its warmth. About half the herd grazes on the short grass. The rest of the steers lie in small groups dotting the hillside like families picnicking in a park.

Kenny and Badger stop and unsaddle their horses before sitting side by side on the ground. Badger chews on a piece of jerky and offers some to Kenny. The cow boss rolls his eyes and declines the half-eaten, drool-covered jerky. Moments after the horses begin grazing, they raise their heads; their ears point west toward the massive mountains. They paw the ground and shift from hoof to hoof. The hairs on the back of Badger's neck rise.

"I don't like what the horses are doin'," Badger says. "It makes me anxious. This is how KB acted last night when the rustlers were trackin' me."

"I don't think we're bein' followed," Kenny says. "I think there's another storm movin' in. Rest quickly, Badger. We'll be pullin' out soon. Storms up this high this time of year tend to drop a lot of snow."

"I've never seen snow in August," Badger says.

"You can feel that chill movin' in, can't you?" Kenny asks.

Badger tightens the scarf around his neck. Then he checks the back of his saddle to make sure his rolled-up raincoat is still there. The young cowboy wonders whether his bedroll in the

52

buckaroo wagon will get wet. He wishes he had another set of clothes in the wagon, just in case he gets soaked through today.

As the herd rests, columns of dark clouds march over the horizon like a cavalry charging its enemies. The gentle breeze whips into a gust.

"Let's move out," Kenny says as he jumps to his feet.

Kenny saddles and mounts his horse. He whistles sharply three times. Gib, Horace, and Percy snap to attention and get back to work. With Kenny and Badger pushing the drag, the herd bunches and moves out. The steers feel the storm moving in, so they walk with fewer grazing breaks.

Buckhorn Ridge spans several miles. Gib and Percy have formed a lead bunch of fifty or so beasts. This small group pulls the rest of the herd along. Horace rides easily behind a second bunch of about one hundred steers. As Badger and Kenny follow the drag, an icy raindrop thuds on the brim of Badger's hat. He looks up, and several drops splatter on his face. Badger dismounts and unties his coat. He puts it on as the rain begins falling steadily. Badger remounts and pulls his coat to his chin.

"It could be worse," Badger says to Kenny. "It could be snowin'."

Kenny doesn't laugh, or even smile. "Those gray clouds comin' down the mountain could be carryin' snow. It just might get worse yet."

The steers are quickly drenched and water

drips off their backs. Their heads hang low, and they tuck their tails tightly behind their backsides to stay warm. They walk with short steps. The temperature drops, and hail replaces the rain.

Clouds shroud the late-morning sun, making it darker than it should be. The short grasses bow in the stiff wind, and the caravan of cowboys and cattle can find no shelter in the treeless landscape. Badger pulls his hat lower to protect his face from the stinging ice. The steers face away from the hail and drop their heads even lower.

"We've gotta keep the steers movin' so we can get off this ridge before the weather turns worse," Kenny yells through the gusts of wind.

KB turns his head away from the pelting ice, but Badger pulls the large horse around to move the herd. KB pins his ears back in protest as the hail smacks him in the face. Each time Badger must zag in the other direction, KB spins quickly and then walks slowly.

The steers barely move despite Badger's and Kenny's shouts. Badger's coat and hat are drenched, and his face stings from the hail.

After thirty minutes, the shower slows, and the ice chunks grow lighter. The steers line out and walk again, moving carefully across the slippery ground.

"I'm glad the storm's over," Badger says, cracking a small smile.

"I'm afraid it's not over, Badger. Are you still dry?" Kenny asks.

"I'm wet on the outside, but it hasn't soaked through yet."

"Good, good. Once you get wet, you'll be cold for days. The only way to stay warm is to keep movin'."

THE STEERS SLOG IN a straight line. From the drag, Badger can't see the steeper trail dropping off the ridge, but Kenny tells him it's close. Snow eventually replaces the hail. The wet flakes carpet the ground and accumulate on the steers' backs and cowboys' shoulders. The beasts look like steer-shaped snowmen. The cowboys brush the snow off their shoulders before it can melt into their coats.

Badger's teeth chatter, and the cold drains his energy. His toes and fingers are numb and tingle painfully. As Badger moves back and forth, he feels a freezing trickle of water race down his spine.

"I just felt the water break through to my skin," Badger tells Kenny.

"Yeah, me too. This is the driest you'll be for the rest of the day, Badger. The only way to stay warm now is to keep movin'. We gotta get these steers to Gordie's campsite, or the cold might overtake us."

Badger hunches his shoulders and fights off a shiver. The snow keeps falling and falling and falling. Water soaks through Badger's clothes. His leather vest, chaps, and boots provide some protection, but even those are getting soggy.

"Herd 'em up, Badger," Kenny says. "The lead steers are startin' down the break in the ridge. When we get to the bottom, we'll find shelter for the cattle and Gordie's campsite for us."

56

Badger's sigh of relief hitches in his throat as he takes in the distance; the trail spans another two miles before it reaches the valley's floor.

"It'll take hours to get down there," Badger whines.

"It's all downhill. The steers'll go fast if we keep pushin' 'em," Kenny says.

The lead steers meander along the trail like paddleboats down a muddy river. They kick up small rocks, which tumble down the ridge. Several steers fall on the steep slope, landing on their knees and sliding a few feet. The mud is soft, though, and the beasts show no signs of pain. Gib and Percy guide their horses carefully on one side of the herd, and Horace rides alone on the other. The cowboys avoid the slick path where the steers have churned up the soil.

"Stay on that side of the herd," Kenny yells to Badger as he points north, "and don't take KB where the steers have walked. They make the hillside even more slippery."

KB edges down the trail, testing the ground's firmness before placing his weight on his legs. Suddenly, Kenny yelps as his horse slips and falls. The horse struggles to rise, but Kenny's weight pins the beast down, and the horse's weight traps Kenny's leg between the animal's massive side and the cold earth.

"Badger! Badger! Badger, help!" Kenny yells.

Badger dismounts and runs toward Kenny, who is about forty feet away. Halfway to the cow boss, Badger slips in the slick mud. He jumps back up and races over. Kenny is bathed in brown goop and winces in pain every time his horse shifts.

"Are you okay?" Badger asks.

"I don't think my leg's broken yet," Kenny says in anguish, "but you gotta get me outta here."

The horse rests for a few seconds and then again struggles in vain to get up. Kenny clenches his teeth, and his face contorts like a baby with a wet diaper.

"Badger, lift up on the saddle horn," Kenny shouts.

"I'll try, but I don't think I'm strong enough," Badger says, his eyes wide and fearful. "Should I go get the others?"

"You can do it, Badger," Kenny assures him. "Put all of your weight into it. I need just a little room so I can crawl out."

Badger leans down and lifts on the saddle horn with all his strength. His stomach feels like it's going to pop out from the strain. His tired legs burn, and his shoulders shift like they're about to burst from their sockets. With Badger pulling, the saddle moves just enough for Kenny to inch his backside up the slope. Without warning, Badger's hands slip.

"Eee yawww!" the seasoned cowboy howls as horse and saddle slump back onto his leg.

"I'm sorry!" Badger cries. "It slipped."

"It's okay, Badger," Kenny replies before inhaling deeply. "Hurry and lift one more time. I'm almost out."

The youngster grabs the saddle horn again

and heaves. Badger's face turns red, and his knees creak. He closes his eyes and focuses all his strength on lifting. Kenny squirms and wiggles until his leg pops free. Then he crawls about five feet like a rattlesnake up a hillside.

"Thanks, Badger," Kenny says between breaths. "I told you that you could do it."

Badger puts his hand on his lower back and stretches his shoulders and neck before responding.

"Why'd you think I could do it, Kenny?" Badger asks. "You haven't noticed me doin' much right up to this point."

Kenny eyes the chubby youngster speculatively.

"You're right, Badger. I had been lookin' for you and your friend Percy to fail," Kenny says in a moment of honesty. "But after you got the herd back yesterday, I started lookin' for you to do things right. I gotta admit, you've changed my outlook on ridin' with kids. I'd trust you watchin' my back anytime."

Badger swallows his surprise and surveys Kenny's leg.

"Are you all right?" he asks.

"I don't think anything's broken. The mud's soft enough that the full weight of him wasn't on my leg. I'll be sore in the mornin', but it's nothin' permanent."

Kenny limps to his horse and checks the beast's hooves and ankles for injuries. The cow boss mounts up and adjusts himself in the saddle. Once settled, Kenny doesn't even hint at his pain.

The two cowboys ride over to the drag and resume pushing the steers down the mountain.

The lead steers finally reach the flat plain about one hundred feet below the top of the ridge and begin grazing as the drag catches up.

Chapter Six

AFTER FORTY-FIVE MINUTES of hard herding through a lighter rain, the steers meander to a wide flat. Gordie has camp set and is cooking rattlesnake, rabbit, and biscuits for lunch. Gordie found an apple tree along his miner trail and offers the fresh fruit to the soaked cowboys.

As the steers fan out and graze, Badger looks around camp like an owl searching for breakfast. *Where are the rustlers?* he wonders as he chomps into a crisp apple.

"Hey, Gordie, how are you?" Badger asks

"Everything is good now, but the road was really steep and slick with rain," Gordie replies as he stirs the meat.

"Where, uh, are the rustlers?" Badger asks as he looks around the campsite once more.

"I let them go."

"You what?" Badger shouts as his eyebrows climb toward his curly, brown bangs.

"I let them go. Is my English incorrect? *Watashi wa karera o tebanasu* ... Yeah, that is right. I let the rustlers go."

"But why? They were worth a lot of reward money to me."

"Fifty dollars at most; probably less. Anyway, the road was slippery, and I needed help getting the wagon down the hill. They agreed to help me if I let them go. Besides, I was tired of their constant complaining. They were—how do you say—driving me crazy."

"But I wanted that reward," Badger says. "Yes, but our first job is to get the steers to Deeth. Our second job is to get home safely. Transporting criminals to the sheriff isn't even on the list of jobs."

"Well, maybe you're right," Badger says as he crawls under the canvas shelter at the back of the buckaroo wagon, "but I still would've liked the reward money. And what if they come back and try to steal the herd again?"

"I don't think they will," Gordie says confidently. "Both were pretty shook up from last night. The one called Joe was still crying about almost getting shot, and the one named Ike still wasn't talking. I think he got hit on the head pretty hard. And I have their guns, so they shouldn't be a threat."

The campfire's heat and a hot cup of coffee help calm Badger's annoyance. The chubby teen

pouts a little bit more as he warms up. Gib, Horace, and Percy dismount, unsaddle, and find a dry spot under the tarp at the back of the wagon. They hold their hands out to the flames as Gordie quickly fills three more cups of coffee.

"Hey, Badger, what happened to your cattle rustlers?" Gib asks as he cozies up to the fire.

"Gordie needed help, so he put the rustlers to work and then let 'em go. I can't believe you just let 'em go!" Badger snaps.

"What else could I do? I didn't want you guys waiting here in the rain when I had two men who could help me move the wagon," Gordie says.

"Gordie is a good cook, but he's not so good as a warden," Gib says as Badger rolls his eyes and chuckles twice.

As the others settle down beneath the tarp, Kenny looks at the clouds and says, "Let's get warm, dry, and fed while it's rainin'. Once this rain stops, we need to make a strong push to get to Deeth in time."

THE RAIN DRIZZLES FOR another hour and then stops. The thirsty soil absorbs the water like a crusty, old sponge. The sandy dirt is still wet, but it's not as slick and mushy. The clouds part, revealing the sun, which looks like a dazzling star posing at center stage as theater curtains whisk open. The cowboys have one more cup of coffee to warm their wet bodies. Their gear is still damp, and they are all chilled. They break camp and scatter to bunch the herd. Gordie drives the buckaroo wagon away down a more wagon-friendly path.

The four hundred steers walk into Canyon

Creek, where the herd disappears into a landscape filled with thick brush and willows. A small creek winds down the wide valley. Willows stand on the creek banks, and sagebrush as tall as a man on horseback fills the rest of the area. All the cowboys ride in the back. They see only the last few steers, but the sagebrush waves back and forth whenever a steer brushes against one. In this way, the cowboys follow the herd.

A small flock of sage grouse jumps out of the sagebrush and flies a short way down the valley. The sudden movement scares the steers, and they take off like mice running from a cat. Gib spurs his horse into action.

"Gib, just wait," Kenny says. "The steers can't leave this valley. Just let 'em settle down."

Gib's muscles loosen, and he easily slips back into the group's pace.

"I hate sage chickens," Percy says, scowling toward the grouse.

"Why's that?" Badger asks with his head tilted.

"They always wait until you're right on top of 'em before they fly away. It's like they're tryin' to spook the steers."

"I like 'em," Badger says. "They're a pretty good meal, and they're easy to shoot."

"But they're so awkward and clumsy," Percy replies. "They flap their wings like crazy just to get off the ground. And then they only fly a few feet. With all that effort, you'd think they could get a little farther."

"But, Percy, that's what makes 'em a good dinner. Try shootin' bluebirds. They never give you a good shot. And if you hit one, there's no meat on its bones."

"I think I like eagles better."

"To eat? Are you crazy?"

"No, Badger, not to eat. I like the way they fly," Percy says as he stretches his arms out. "I like the way they soar. Someday, I'd like to ride as graceful as an eagle."

"Till we learn how to keep our backsides in the saddle, we both ride like a couple of sage chickens," Badger replies with a laugh.

The older men snort and chuckle their agreement.

THE COWBOYS PUSH THE steers out of Canyon Creek. The landscape around the trail changes as they ride. The sandy soil is peppered with rocks like meatballs on a hill of spaghetti. The steers graze on short grasses in between patches of small sagebrush. Little hills roll up and down for miles like a stormy ocean. The herd moves south on the trail down to Camp Creek, where the steers stop to graze and rest on a thick carpet of grass. Gordie has the buckaroo wagon parked, and he is cooking three sage chickens and biscuits. The coffee bubbles as it boils. Kenny rides up and scopes out the campsite.

"Let's rest here for the afternoon. The steers are tired. They're not goin' anywhere," Kenny says as he surveys the herd. "Tomorrow might be a long day."

We're about to Deeth, aren't we?" Badger asks.

"We're about a day and a half out," Horace says.

"I don't see any more mountains or canyons. How hard could this last part be?" Badger asks.

"The desert is flat but it's dry. We might have a hard time findin' water."

"What do you mean, Horace? How far is the next water?" Badger asks.

"It might be just over the next hill in Sun Creek, but that's probably dry. There aren't too many creeks or springs or even seeps between here and Deeth. And this late in the season, they're most likely dry. The next water is apt to be the Humboldt River just outside Deeth."

"But it rained and snowed today," Badger protests. "How can the creeks be dry?"

"Did you see any of that water runnin'? It all went into the ground. If we're lucky, it'll come outta the springs next year."

"What about the water barrel on the buckaroo wagon? That should give us some water," Badger says.

"Gordie fills it up every time he crosses a creek," Horace replies. "But it's barely enough water for cookin' and for us to drink. We'll have four hundred thirsty steers plus our horses to water. They don't make water barrels that big."

Badger tips his hat back and runs his fingers through his hair. This cattle drive has been one surprise after another. He cracks a smile like a gambler whose bluff has been called.

"Don't worry about it tonight, Badger. Get some rest for tomorrow," Horace says.

"You want me to not worry, knowin' we won't see water again for a day and a half? I don't think I'll be able to sleep too well," Badger says.

BADGER AND PERCY STRETCH their bedrolls out on the hard dirt before yanking off their boots and hats and stripping off their vests and chaps. The boys keep their other clothes on, though, to help them stay warm. They pull the blankets tight, looking like swaddled newborns. Their bellies are full of sage chicken, biscuits, and gooseberry pie.

Horace is already deep asleep, snoring like a rooting pig. Kenny saddles his horse so he can check on the herd one more time. Meanwhile, Gordie washes pots, and Gib—eyes closed—plays his harmonica.

"When did you learn to play the harmonica?" Percy asks Gib.

The well-kempt cowboy finishes his chorus and takes a breath before replying.

"My mother taught me to play the piano when I was younger. I could play a song just from listenin' to it," Gib says. "Anyway, when I started cowboyin', I missed the music. After my first drive, I got paid and bought a shiny, new harmonica. I like the simple tunes it makes. And I have the crickets' and night birds' chirpin' to accompany me. I also like the way a little harmonica can scare away the loneliness of the night."

"How long have you been cowboyin'?"

Percy asks.

"About six years," Gib says. "I was your age when I started. I was just as green as you are."

"How long until we can ride as well as you?" Badger asks.

"It took me a long time. The hardest part about ridin' is keepin' your backside in the saddle. I even have trouble with that now on occasion. If you guys keep at it, you'll get better."

Kenny rides away and shouts over his shoulder, "The steers are bedded down, so no night watch tonight. Get some sleep. We've got a long day tomorrow."

"We always have a long day tomorrow," Badger moans.

Percy and Gib laugh. Kenny cracks a smile as he turns down the trail.

MILLIONS OF STARS DOT the clear night sky. They twinkle like sunlight on snowdrifts. Badger pulls his itchy blanket around his neck. His head is chilly, and a cold ache seizes his body. The night is too cold for crickets, so the darkness is silent. He stares at the stars and pulls his arms closer to his body for warmth. After blinking twice more, he takes a deep breath and falls into a restless sleep.

Chapter Seven

BADGER OPENS HIS EYES and sees the sun lazily climbing above the eastern mountains. He blinks twice and jumps out of his bedroll. The frosty morning bites at Badger's nose and ears. Gib walks to the horses to round them up. Gordie stands over a pot of biscuits and a mysterious slab of meat.

"Mornin', Badger," Kenny says.

"Mornin'," Badger replies, intentionally avoiding the phrase "good mornin'."

"Wake up, Percy," Badger says as he shakes his friend.

"I'm awake; I'm awake," Percy says without getting out of his bedroll. "I'm just tryin' to warm up."

"What's for breakfast?" Badger asks, looking at the roasting meat.

"Jackrabbit," Gordie replies. "I can only find

rabbits and rattlesnakes in this valley. We'll probably have rattlesnake for lunch."

"I can hardly wait," Badger says with a sarcastic smile.

"Rabbit tastes pretty good once you get used to it."

"I don't wanna get used to it," Badger grumbles.

Nonetheless, the youngster grabs a plate and eats his breakfast like a hungry drifter. As he downs a cup of dark, foul-tasting coffee, Badger's nose scrunches and the corners of his mouth curl downward. He wants to spit, but the fresh-faced cowboy forces the hot liquid down. He washes his plate and rinses his cup in the nearby stream.

Badger grabs his bridle and catches KB. As usual, the brown beast has his ears pinned back, looking as mad as ever. *KB is grouchier in the mornin' than Horace*, Badger thinks, chuckling to himself. Badger throws his saddle on KB's back and pulls the cinch tight around the horse's chest.

As Horace and Percy finish eating, Gib walks his young horse in a tight circle to calm him. Kenny mounts his horse and turns back to the cowboys.

"I'm goin' to UC Ranch to ask where the next water is. It's just down the valley, and I shouldn't be long," the cow boss says. "Gib and Badger, head on out and get the herd bunched up and movin' south. Horace and Percy, help Gordie pack the wagon; then catch up to the herd as quick as you can."

Kenny departs with his final command. "Are you ready to go?" Gib asks Badger. Badger swings onto KB and nods.

All horses are antsy on a cold morning, but Gib's colt is even more so because of his age. Gib circles his red roan one more time. He adjusts the reins from the ground, places his foot in the stirrup, and swings into the saddle. Gib adjusts his seat and readjusts the reins. He pulls the young horse's head around and gently pushes his spur in his mount's side.

The colt jumps uncomfortably to the side. Gib responds by kicking him gently with the other spur. Gib's horse stubbornly pulls his head away. The cowboy pulls it around again, but the colt flinches in the other direction. The young mount rears back on his hind legs and shakes his head from left to right. Gib's face shows no fear, but his uneasy horse circles and shakes his head again.

The colt lunges forward and drops his head close to the ground as his front feet hit the earth. Gib absorbs the first jump like his backside is glued to the saddle. The horse jumps to the left and bucks with all his might. Gib sits calmly on top of the chaos. The duo lunges toward the buckaroo wagon and campfire. The beast bucks the forty feet to the campfire in three powerful jumps. Horace and Percy jump to their feet. Percy launches himself to the side and runs about twenty feet away. Horace dashes two steps and then walks to safety. Gordie watches the whole incident from beneath the buckaroo wagon.

The horse jumps into the middle of the smoldering campfire. Sparks fly in all directions, but Gib stubbornly stays in his saddle. The colt catches his front hoof on the pot of biscuits. He trips and falls to his front knees. Gib seems like he is cinched to his saddle. The roan stands and pants heavily. Gib readjusts his seat and then the reins.

Then he jabs both spurs into the colt. The horse runs quickly, and Gib reins him to the left and right to be sure he is in control. Gib rides down the valley about a quarter mile and then returns to camp.

As he approaches the wagon, he looks at Gordie and says without stopping, "Sorry 'bout breakfast, Gordie."

"No problem," Gordie responds with a smile.

"Ready to go, Badger?" Gib asks.

"I'm just waitin' for you," Badger replies.

As they leave, Gib looks to Badger and says, "This is a bad sign. I don't like the way today started. It's gonna be a bad day."

Badger smiles and says, "Maybe for you. My horse didn't buck, so I'm plannin' on a good day."

"Well, we can hope, but I don't like its start," Gib says with a scowl.

THE STEERS WALK QUICKLY as the plain opens in front of them. Sagebrush stands about knee-high, and greenish-yellow grass fills in the spaces between the clumps of brush. The herd kicks

up thick, white dust. Badger's eyes burn from the ·
bright sun and gritty dirt. About ten o'clock, the sun
warms Badger for the first time in more than a day.
The young cowboy basks in the rays as he moves
back and forth behind the herd. By ten-thirty,
Badger is sweating. The cowboys stop to pull off
their coats and tie them to the back of their saddles.
They take off their scarves and retie them loosely.

At lunchtime, all the cowboys avoid the
campfire. They pick at their food like vultures
approaching a week-old carcass. They drink stale
water from the barrel at the side of the wagon.

"Everybody, water up," Kenny says. "This
may be your last chance to get water till tomorrow."

"Why? Doesn't Gordie carry an extra barrel
of water with him?" Badger asks. "Then we
wouldn't have to worry about runnin' out."

"Water in a barrel goes bad pretty fast out
here," Kenny says. "He could carry extra water, but
it would just make you sick. Bein' thirsty is just part
of bein' a cowboy."

Gib and Horace sip the stale water. Badger
and Percy fill their cups and guzzle.

"Be careful, boys," Horace warns. "Drinkin'
too fast can give you a bellyache."

The two boys slow their slurping but still fill
their stomachs. They sit on the grass and rub their
full bellies. Badger inhales and swallows hard.

"I think I drank too much," he says with a
grimace.

"Me too. I wish I could take a nap to let my
lunch settle," Percy replies sourly.

76

Badger and Percy waddle to their horses. The mixture of food and water sloshes with every step. They mount their horses and sway from side to side to keep their lunch from splashing around. Horace and Gib have corralled the wandering herd, and the steers line out to travel. Badger and Percy get to work, but they are as uncomfortable as gorged ticks.

The sun glares over the low plain. As the herd heads into the lower elevations of O'Neil Basin, the desert air grows thicker and hotter. The steers pant with the building heat. Fewer steers stray to eat, but all of them walk more slowly. The sun strolls slowly across the afternoon sky, endlessly beating down on the herd. The farther south they travel, the hotter the glare becomes. The cowboys sweat until about four o'clock when their sweat glands run dry.

"I stopped sweatin'," Badger says as he passes Percy in the drag.

Percy looks up and nods, but he says nothing.

"I'm still hot, though," Badger confides, "and I don't see anythin' that looks like a creek or spring. I could really use a nap, too."

Percy looks at Badger again but keeps his mouth closed. The scrawny teen's face is drawn downward, and his lips quiver. Misery laps at Percy like the waves of heat engulfing the desert. The sizzling temperatures and sand make the young cowboy's eyes burn. He's so hot and tired, he'd probably cry if he had any moisture left to give to the August day. Percy swallows hard. He turns from Badger and moves the steers in front of him. Snowball and KB are struggling, too. The heat stresses their weary muscles, and dehydration makes their joints ache.

   THE SUN SINKS LOWER, but there's still no water or shade in sight. Typically, the cowboys would be settling the steers and allowing them to drink and graze; but that isn't an option now. The steers could eat the short, brown grass, but their intense thirst drives the beasts' hunger away. So the group continues to amble along the bleak, treeless trail.

   Kenny moves back to the drag. He acts like a fireman in a boiler room, showing no strain from the heat and lack of water. Kenny rides with a bounce in his horse's step and a small smile. His eyes tighten slightly as he surveys the boys.

   He frowns and asks, "How are you two holdin' up?"

   Percy looks at him and nods.

   Badger says, "We're pretty rough, but we're keepin' up."

   "You two are doin' a good job. I appreciate your effort. From now on, let's slow the herd down. We'll keep 'em movin', but let's not push 'em too hard. Without water, the steers won't settle until dark. You should get off your horses and air their backs from time to time, too. Once the sun goes down, we'll stop and rest for a couple hours. Gordie drove the wagon on ahead to set up camp, but we won't really stop for the night till we reach water."

"Did the folks at UC Ranch know where the next water is?" Badger asks.

"They said it's real dry south of here. Sun Creek is empty, and most of the springs are dry," Kenny answers with a sigh. "They haven't been past Tabor Creek, but they heard it's dry, too. We just gotta keep herdin' 'em till we get to Humboldt River."

"We'll keep 'em movin'," Badger says.

Percy looks at Kenny and nods his agreement. He still looks like he might cry.

As the sun touches the western mountains, the heat fizzles out and the herd settles down. Badger is thirsty, but the cool air helps. The teen licks his dry tongue across his cracked lips. Kenny dismounts, pulls the saddle off his horse, and lies on the ground. Horace and Gib follow his lead. Moments later, Badger and Percy mimic the older cowboys. The steers stop and chew on the brittle grass. After a few minutes of grazing, many lie down and rest their weary muscles.

AS THE SUN DISAPPEARS behind the horizon, dusk creeps across the desert. Gordie has made camp. He stands over a pot, checking its contents.

"What's for dinner, Gordie?" Badger asks as he ambles over to the wagon.

"There isn't much game around here. Tonight will be just jerky and biscuits," Gordie says with his head bowed. "I don't even have enough water for coffee. Sorry, it's the best I can do."

"It's okay, Gordie. None of us is really hungry," Kenny lies, trying to make Gordie feel better.

The cowboys eat quickly and settle down to nap. Badger is tired, but his thirst makes him restless. Percy falls right to sleep despite Horace snoring like an off-key bagpipe. Kenny and Gib toss and turn, but they can't get to sleep either. As the waning full moon peaks high above the cowboys,

Kenny and Gib slither around like snakes in a blanket. Percy and Horace move only to breathe.

"Who can't sleep?" Kenny asks quietly.

"I can't," Gib replies.

"I'm wide awake," Badger says with a huff. "The steers aren't beddin' down either," Kenny says. "I'm gettin' up to keep the herd bunched up. If anybody wants to join me, I could sure use the help."

"I'll help," Gib says. "It'd be good to get a little bit closer."

"I'm too hungry and thirsty to sleep, so I might as well pitch in," Badger says.

Gordie rises and says, "If I can borrow a horse, I'll help, too."

"You can use Percy's horse, Gordie. We could really use your help," Kenny says.

Percy and Horace sleep like dead men. Kenny pulls out a pad of paper, writes a quick note to the slumbering cowboys, and pins it to a wagon shelf. The others saddle horses and walk to the herd. They make quiet noises to warn the edgy beasts. The anxious steers group quickly and start heading

80

south. The moon provides some light, but the cowboys rely on their horses' eyes to find their way in the night as the steers continue searching for water.

Badger is miserable. He is tired, and his stomach is knotted with hunger. His lips are dry and cracked, and his swollen tongue feels like a cotton ball. His eyes ache from lack of sleep and dehydration. His nose is raw and sunburned. *At least the darkness helps the soreness*, Badger thinks. *But poor Percy looks as dried out as a raisin. I hope he's all right.*

Gordie and Badger pass back and forth behind the herd. They avoid sudden movements and noises that might startle the steers. They sing mumbled songs to let the herd know where they are. Gordie sings in Japanese. The lyrics are mysterious, and the tune is foreign to Badger's ears. Badger rasps out a song he remembers his father singing years back:

> *Snackin' on snakes to keep from starvin,*
> *Crackin' a smile to keep from cryin',*
> *Pushin' these steers to earn my livin',*
> *Way out west in no man's land.*

> *Wakin' up cold most every mornin',*
> *Beggin' for water to cool my dry lips,*
> *Chokin' on dust and always dirty,*
> *Way out west in no man's land.*

> *Keep on wakin' up each mornin',*
> *Keep on pushin' up this mountain,*
> *Keepin' the trail long behind me,*
> *Makin' my way in no man's land.*

81

Badger's voice wavers and cracks as he rides in the darkness. He envies Gib and his harmonica as the tune of a beautiful waltz carries from somewhere ahead.

AS DAWN GRAYS THE eastern horizon, the cowboys dismount, and the steers lie down. The gray melts into dull orange before bursting into vibrant pink. As the sun pokes over the horizon, a still blue creeps across the sky, and Horace and Percy crest the northern hill in the buckaroo wagon. Gordie mounts up and rides to the wagon. Horace and Percy make their way to the herd. Badger notices that Percy looks even more pale and thin, and Horace is more pleasant than usual this morning. With everyone tired and thirsty, Badger wonders if Horace is bottling his customary complaints to keep from making the cowboys feel worse.

"How you feelin', Percy?" Badger asks.

"I'm so hungry even rattlesnake sounds good. We're in the desert; couldn't we at least find a rattlesnake?" Percy replies pathetically.

"Rattlesnakes need water just like everythin' else, Percy," Horace says. "They get thirsty, and they eat little critters that rely on water. If you find your rattlesnake, water'll be close by."

Percy shakes his head and looks at the ground. Badger pats him on the shoulder and settles down on the hard earth beside his friend. Gordie drives the buckaroo wagon around the herd and follows the trail south.

"Where's Gordie goin'?" Percy asks.

"Without water, he can't cook biscuits,"

Horace says, "and he can't find any game. So I guess he's goin' on ahead to water."

Percy and Badger watch as Gordie and his mules top the far ridge. *Gordie'll be the first to get a drink*, Badger thinks with a surge of jealousy, *while we're starin' at the north end of south-bound steers.* Just before Gordie drops out of sight, his rifle flashes and a thunderous shot cracks throughout the valley. The steers get to their feet but do not stampede. Gordie jumps down from his wagon, picks up something off the ground, and waves it above his head excitedly.

"*Gara-gara heibe! Gara-gara heibe!*" Gordie yells frantically.

"What's he sayin'?" Badger asks.

"I can't make it out," Horace replies.

"I think he's gone crazy," Percy says. "The thirst has messed with his brain."

"*GARA-GARA HEIBE! GARA-GARA HEIBE!*" Gordie shouts as he dances a quick jig.

"He always speaks in Japanese when he's excited," Horace says.

Kenny rides over to Gordie. After a brief talk, Kenny gallops to Gib, and then Gib gallops to the drag. Gib has a smile plastered across his face like a miner who has just seen color.

He laughs and says, "Gara-gara heibe! It's Japanese for rattlesnake. Gordie shot a rattlesnake. And if there's a rattlesnake here—"

"Then water's close by," Horace interrupts. "Let's get these steers up and move 'em to water!"

The tired and thirsty cowboys swing onto their horses. With a burst of borrowed energy, they trot their mounts behind the steers. The herd walks slowly, though, lacking the cowboys' enthusiasm. The team urges, yells, and spooks, but nothing inspires the beasts to move.

"Save your energy, boys," Horace says with a sigh. "It looks like a slow walk is the steers' top speed right now. We know we're close. We just gotta be patient."

Percy and Badger settle into their routine of moving back and forth. Despite Horace's advice, they scowl and yell at the stubborn steers. They plead and beg, but it does no good. The morning is crisp and cool but dry. A thick cloud of dust hangs in the air long after the herd has moved.

As the lead steers crest the next hill, they stampede wildly. The trailing steers follow them. The herd finally discovers what the cowboys have known for an hour. They lumber swiftly to the bottom of a green valley, where a river cuts through a lush meadow. Badger and Percy ride toward the upstream portion of the river, where Kenny and Gib are already off their horses and getting drinks. Horace dismounts and saunters over as Badger and Percy streak past him to the water's edge. The young cowboys lie on their bellies with their heads over the riverbank, sucking water into their mouths like camels at an oasis.

"Slow down, boys," Kenny says. "If you drink too fast, you'll get cramps. We'll stay here for the rest of the day, so take several small drinks."

Gordie sets up camp. He adds two rabbits to the rattlesnake he shot, and soon steam rises from grilling meat. It is slightly brown, and its aroma has the cowboys' mouths watering. A batch of biscuits is browning in a pot next to the fire, and the coffeepot hisses like a steam-engine locomotive.

The steers drink heartily. Some remain in the water, while others eat like wolves over a fresh kill.

"Should we keep the herd together?" Percy asks Kenny.

"No, let 'em graze," the cow boss replies. "They gotta make up for havin' empty stomachs yesterday."

The cowboys feast on the meat and biscuits. Badger no longer complains about eating rattlesnake as the meat's flavor dances across his tongue. The biscuits are piping hot, and Badger happily licks a few stray golden flakes off his fingers. Gordie offers freshly picked gooseberries to the cowboys, who wolf them down by the handful. The juice from the sweet, little berries tickles their taste buds and eases their rough throats.

"We have plenty of coffee," Gordie reminds them

They all shake their heads no.

"I plan on takin' a nap after I eat," Badger says around a mouthful of delicious biscuit. "I don't need any coffee this mornin'. I wanna get rested up. There's no tellin' what other problems we'll see between here and Deeth."

Kenny and Horace laugh.

85

"I don't think we'll have any more problems," Kenny says.

Badger furrows his brow and tilts his head to the right.

"After all we've seen in the past four days, surely somethin' else is gonna go wrong," Badger says.

"Deeth is just over this hill, Badger," Gib replies. "It's about a three-hour drive from here."

"We'll let the steers fill up on grass and water before we go on down," Kenny says. "But Badger, we made it, and you'll get your money. We made it thanks to your help."

As the cowboys' assurances sink in, Badger reflects on the mishaps, the thunderstorm, the rustlers, the snow, the heat, and the drought. Then the youngster grins broadly as he settles down to a long and refreshing nap.

buckaroo—From the Spanish word vaquero. A buckaroo is someone who works with cattle and horses, especially in the far Western United States.

bunch (the herd)—The act of encouraging cattle to form a herd or gather as a group.

cinch—a strap that is attached to a saddle and looped around a horses chest. When pulled tight, the cinch holds the saddle in place.

corral—an enclosure, typically made of wood. It is generally used to hold livestock inside.

corralled—The act of enclosing a herd of cattle or horses. It can be used figuratively to describe cowboys encircling a herd of cattle or horses.

drag—the back of a herd of cattle. Two or more cowboys will ride behind the drag and encourage stragglers to move.

draw—a steep sided valley. May also describe a shallow canyon.

line out—After a group of cattle gathers to a herd, a lead steer emerges and the remaining herd follows.

point—the front of the herd. At least one cowboy will ride at the point to ensure the herd moves in the correct direction.

punchin' cows—herding cows. The act of a cow puncher. Other synonyms: buckaroo, cowboy, cowhand, cowman, cowpoke, drover, waddie, and wrangler.

push the edges—between the point and the drag are the edges. At least one cowboy will ride at the side of the herd to move the middle of the herd forward.

rough string—describes the most difficult horses to ride. These horses are young, mean, or untrained and will buck and be difficult to ride. The most skilled rider will typically ride this group of horses.

rounds the herd—with a stopped herd, a rider will walk slowly around the herd to keep them together. Rounding the herd is this act.

rustled, rustler—describes the act of stealing cattle. A rustler is someone who steals cattle.

saddle—made of leather stretched tightly on a wooden frame. The saddle is placed on the back of a horse and is the seat where a cowboy rides

saddle horn—a small, short post on the front of the saddle. The post can be used by the rider to maintain balance.

sagebrush—a greenish bush found throughout the intermountain west. Sagebrush can be as small as a few inches and as tall as ten feet.

sage chicken—More commonly called a sage grouse. A sage chicken is a medium sized bird. Similar to a domestic chicken, the sage grouse has limited flight capabilities.

stirrup—A part of a saddle. A riders foot is placed in the stirrup when the rider is mounted. The stirrup aids in balance and when used properly will bind the rider to the horse.

wrangle—the act of gathering a herd of horses.

Badger Thurston and the Cattle Drive is a work of fiction. But aspects of this book are based on real history. The area described in this book is on the border of Idaho and Nevada. To market their cattle, early ranchers would band together to get their cattle over the Jarbidge Mountains and to the nearest railroad station in Deeth, Nevada.

In 1910, a group of cowboys made the drive from Southern Idaho to Deeth and documented their trip with a photograph in Elko, Nevada upon completion of this drive. My great grandfather was part of that journey and was part of the picture. He rode over much of the same area described in this book.

Cattle ranching is still a vital part of this area today. I have made the trip over the mountains described in this book several times. I have never encountered cattle rustlers. But I have experienced rain, wind, cold, hail, snow, heat, drought, and thirst, often all on the same trip. Even today I will encounter stubborn steers, unruly horses, rattlesnakes, sage chickens, and ill tempered cowboys. Even when my muscles ache and I have sores from my saddle, I remember how lucky I am to ride the range and the same routes that my great- grandfather rode.

About the author...

Gus Brackett was raised on a working cattle ranch in the wide open spaces of Southwestern Idaho and Northeastern Nevada. He was on the back of a horse by the age of five and sold his first steer at the age of ten. Gus was enrolled in a one-room school house where he first started writing stories about cowboys.

As a boy, Gus listened to tall tales about early cowboys from Grandpa Noy Brackett, Uncle Rolly Patrick and Truman Clark. Gus was fascinated by these stories and started writing the Badger Thurston series in 2010 to chronicle these tales.

Gus currently lives and works on the same ranch where he was raised. He is the Chairman of the Board of the one room school where he first wrote cowboy stories. He lives in a little ranch house with his wife Kimberly, four children, and a barn full of horses, steers, dogs, cats, and chickens. He is still writing so look for other books in this series.